# Dear Parent/Caregiver:

Learning to read is one of the most important things a child will ever do. And now, with a little help from that silly old bear, Pooh, learning to read is easy and fun. Using only twelve vocabulary words, Pooh's Readables are the very simplest readers you will find!

With Pooh's Readables, your emerging reader will:

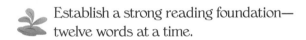 Establish a strong reading foundation—twelve words at a time.

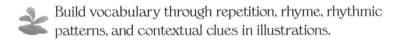 Build vocabulary through repetition, rhyme, rhythmic patterns, and contextual clues in illustrations.

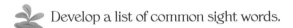 Develop a list of common sight words.

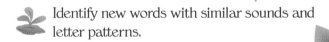 Identify new words with similar sounds and letter patterns.

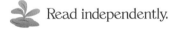 Read independently.

Most important of all, your child will have fun! Silly singsong stories will have your child laughing and learning every step of the way.

# Random House 🏠 New York

Copyright © 2006 Disney Enterprises, Inc. Based on the "Winnie the Pooh" works, by A. A. Milne and E. H. Shepard.
All rights reserved under International and Pan-American Copyright Conventions. Published in the United States
by Random House Children's Books, a division of Random House, Inc., New York, and simultaneously in Canada
by Random House of Canada Limited, Toronto, in conjunction with Disney Enterprises, Inc.
www.randomhouse.com/kids/disney

Library of Congress Cataloging-in-Publication Data

Lagonegro, Melissa.
Grow, seeds, grow! / by Melissa Lagonegro.
p. cm. — (Pooh's readables)

Summary: When Pooh and Piglet plant a garden, they learn from Rabbit
what it takes to make it grow. Focuses on twelve specific words.

ISBN: 0-7364-2353-2

[1. Gardens—Fiction. 2. Teddy Bears—Fiction. 3. Toys—Fiction. 4. Stories in rhyme.]
I. Title. II. Series.
PZ8.3.L214Gr 2006
[E]—dc22
2004023533

MANUFACTURED IN CHINA   10 9 8 7 6 5 4 3 2 1

# Grow, Seeds, Grow!

### By Melissa Lagonegro
Illustrated by the Disney Storybook Artists

Weeds, weeds.
Pull weeds.

Seeds, seeds.
Plant seeds.

# Will seeds grow?

Seeds need sun.
Sun, sun, sun.

Weeds, weeds.
Pull more weeds.

Seeds, seeds.
Plant more seeds.

# Will seeds grow?

No, no, no.

Seeds need rain.
Rain, rain, rain.

# Will seeds grow?

# Grow, seeds. Grow!

Seeds have sun.

# Seeds have rain.

Seeds will grow!
Grow! Grow! Grow!

# Plants!

Here are the twelve
words you just read:

| | |
|---|---|
| weeds | no |
| pull | need |
| seeds | sun |
| plant | more |
| will | rain |
| grow | have |